MW01618425

LIZARD
and the
PAINTED ROCK
Written by Elizabeth Lane
Illustrated by Jim Madsen

The artist had been at work all day. At night the animals came to see what he had painted on the side of the rocky cliff.

"Look," said Rabbit. "The artist has painted me right here. I must be very important."

"Look," said Turtle. "The artist has painted me over here. I must be very important, too."

Lizard looked at the wonderful painted rock. He looked and looked for a picture of a lizard, but he could not find one.

“The artist didn’t paint you, Lizard,” said Rabbit.
“You must not be very important,” said Turtle.
“I guess not,” Lizard said sadly.

Rabbit and Turtle went off to play in the cool, dark night. But Lizard stayed by the painted rock, looking and thinking.

"Why didn't the artist paint me?" he asked the shining moon. "I am just as important as Turtle and Rabbit."

Then he saw something. The artist had left his brush and a small pot of paint near the rock. Suddenly Lizard had an idea.

"I know!" he said. "I will paint my own picture!
Then everyone will know that I am important, too!"

Lizard tried to paint. He tried his best, but nothing he painted looked like a lizard. The paint dripped off the brush and ran down the rock.

Lizard stepped in the paint and got a little of it on his feet. Where he walked, he left painted lizard tracks behind him.

The tracks gave Lizard a new idea. “Ho!” he said. “There’s more than one way to paint a picture!”

Lizard poured some paint on the ground. He crawled around in the paint until the front of him was covered from head to tail.

Then he backed away from the rock. He counted to four and took a long, running leap. *SPLAT!* Lizard's painted body hit the rock…and stuck.

"Help!" Lizard yelled. "I can't get loose!"

Rabbit and Turtle came running. But Lizard had leaped high on the rock. Even when Rabbit stood on Turtle's back, they could not reach him.

Poor Lizard. He knew what would happen if he could not get loose. The morning sun would shine on the rock. Its heat would dry the paint and shrivel his small lizard body. He would be part of the rock forever.

The night was long and sad. Just as the sun was rising, the artist came back.

"What is this?" he asked, laughing. "Today I was going to paint a lizard. Now I see that the lizard has painted himself!"

Very gently, he pulled Lizard loose. Then he looked at the lizard shape the paint had left on the rock. He looked and he thought. "I know," he said at last. "I know what this lizard needs."

He dipped his brush into a new pot of paint. Carefully he made four stripes on the back of the painted lizard.

Then he reached down and painted the same four stripes on Lizard's back. "Now I have truly painted you, Little Brother," he said.

Lizard scurried away,
feeling very, very important.